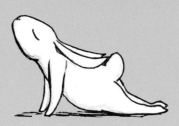   

Upward Dog   Forward Fold   Half Pigeon   half Lift

Chair Pose   Reverse Warrior   Power Lunge   Power Lunge Reach

Thunderbolt   Prayer Twist   Crescent Lunge   Superhero Pose

Butterfly   Happy Baby Pose   Resting Pose

ISBN 978-0-06-242952-0 (trade bdg.)

The artist used colored pencils, watercolor, and Adobe Photoshop to create the digital illustrations for this book.
Typography by Jeanne L. Hogle
16   17   18   19   20   SCP   10   9   8   7   6   5   4   3   2   1
❖
First Edition

for my dad

YOGA BUNNY

by Brian Russo

HARPER
An Imprint of HarperCollinsPublishers

One morning, Bunny crawled out of his hole,
rubbed his eyes, and let out a big YAWN!
"This is a perfect morning to do yoga!" he said.

Bunny dropped his head and arms

down toward his feet

coming into a
forward fold.

Just then, Lizard came walking by.

"Good morning, Lizard," said Bunny.
"Would you like to do yoga with me?"

"I hate everything about mornings! I wish I could go back
to bed," Lizard replied angrily.

And with that, Lizard stomped away.

Bunny was disappointed,
but he took a deep breath,

placed his hands
on the ground,
stepped backward,

and lifted his hips high up in the air,
coming into **downward dog**.

His friend Fox came hurrying by.

Zoom, zoom, zoom!

He was moving so fast, he startled Bunny.
"Out of my way, Bunny," he said. "I'm in a very big rush!"

"Maybe you could take a minute and do
this yoga pose with me," Bunny suggested.
"It might help you slow down."

"No thanks!" Fox replied. "I'd rather be in a big rush than do something so silly."

And he hurried away.

Bunny felt a little bit sad,
but he took a deep breath,
stood up tall,

placed his hands
in front of his heart,

and balanced on one foot,
coming into **tree pose**.

Just then, Bird flew down, landing right on Bunny's head.

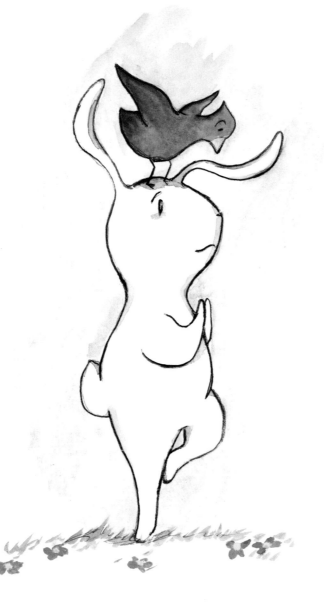

"HICCUP! I have a bad case of the HICCUPS,
and I've tried everything to stop them," said Bird.

"Well," Bunny said. "Maybe you can do this **tree pose** with me. It can calm you down, and that might help with your—"

"HICCUP! No way!" Bird said. "I'd rather live with these hiccups than stand on one leg."

And with that, Bird flew away.

"Will anyone ever want to do yoga with me?"
Bunny wondered aloud. But then he reminded himself
that doing yoga alone is better than not doing yoga at all.

Just as Bunny took a deep breath, stepped back, bent his front leg, and reached his arms way up, coming into **warrior pose**, two little mice came walking by.

"What do you think he's reaching for?" whispered one of the mice.

"I don't know, but it must be very valuable. We'd better reach for it too."

And so the mice stepped back, bent their front legs, and reached their arms way up, coming into **warrior pose**, just like Bunny.

As they had their arms stretched way up and their
eyes toward the sky, they noticed Bird flying by.

Bird still had the hiccups, but he came down to join them,
pressing his wings together in front of his heart, lifting up one leg,
coming into **tree pose**, just like Bunny and the mice.

All of a sudden, they heard a loud noise.

zoom, zoom, zoom!

Fox came hurrying by and saw the friends standing in a circle, and he pressed his hands to the ground, stepped back, and lifted his hips, coming into **downward dog**,

just like Bunny,

the mice,

and Bird.

Bunny took a deep breath and lay down
flat on his back, coming into **resting pose**,

when Lizard came walking back
and lay down just like Bunny.

Bunny was so happy his friends had joined him
that he opened his mouth and let out a big

"OMMMM...."

And everyone else did the same.

"I know where I'm supposed to be," said Fox, not so angry anymore. "It's here."

"Thank you, Yoga Bunny!"

SOME FACTS ABOUT YOGA

The word *yoga* comes from an ancient language called Sanskrit, and it means "connection" or "union," as in "connect your thoughts to your body," "connect your mind to your breath," or "connect your booty to your mat."

The name of one of the most popular forms of yoga, hatha, comes from the words *ha*, meaning "sun," and *tha*, which means "moon." Have you ever been to the moon?

It's unknown how long ago the practice of yoga actually began, but most scientists think it started between five and ten thousand years ago. Did dinosaurs practice yoga? Probably not. It'd be tough for a *T. rex* to do downward dog with those tiny arms!

Many popular yoga poses are based on the stories of Hindu gods and goddesses. For example, the warrior poses are all about the powerful Lord Shiva.

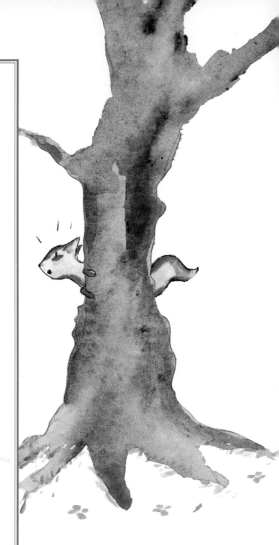

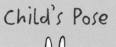
Child's Pose

Downward Dog

Upper Pushup

Lower Pushup

Mountain Pose

Tree Pose

Warrior 1

Warrior 2

Side Angle

Extended Side

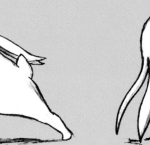

Revolved

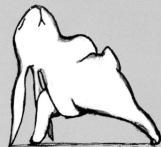
Bound Side Angle

Camel Pose

Seated
Forward Fold

Boat Pose

Bicycle Crunch